crazy stories

BriLLianT Bones

crazy stories

BriLLianT Bones

Written and illustrated by Alexander Brown

© Alexander Brown 2007
First published 2007
ISBN 978 184427 263 1

Scripture Union, 207–209 Queensway, Bletchley, Milton Keynes, MK2 2EB, UK
Email: info@scriptureunion.org.uk
Website: www.scriptureunion.org.uk

Scripture Union Australia, Locked Bag 2, Central Coast Business Centre, NSW 2252, Australia
Website: www.scriptureunion.org.au

Scripture Union USA, PO Box 987, Valley Forge, PA 19482, USA
Website: www.scriptureunion.org

Scripture quotation is taken from the Contemporary English Version © American Bible Society. Anglicisations © British and Foreign Bible Society 1996. Published by HarperCollins*Publishers*.

British Library Cataloguing-in-Data.
A catalogue record of this book is available from the British Library.

Printed and bound by Tien Wah Press, Singapore
Cover design by Kevin Wade, kwgraphicdesign

Scripture Union is an international charity working with churches in more than 130 countries, providing resources to bring the good news of Jesus Christ to children, young people and families and to encourage them to develop spiritually through the Bible and prayer.

As well as our network of volunteers, staff and associates who run holidays, church-based events and school Christian groups, we produce a wide range of publications and support those who use our resources through training programmes.

For Thomas

Harriet Carbuncle Petrifee Jones
had an enormous collection of bones.

Most of her friends thought her terribly weird.
Some of them laughed at her strangeness, and jeered.

Harriet snubbed them, and held her head high,
dreaming of all the dead bones she could buy.

Her first ever memory of bone collecting
began with her Scottish friend, Angus McTeckting.
The two friends were walking along by his loch,
when Angus spied something just next to a rock.

"It looks like a bone," he said. He was right.
When Harriet touched it she buzzed with delight,
right from the tips of her toes to her hair,
and all she could do was just dribble, and stare!

"Look, how amazing, a leg-bone!" she said,
as strange new emotions arose in her head.
She took it straight home, where she showed it around.
"What a wonderful yellowy bone I have found!"

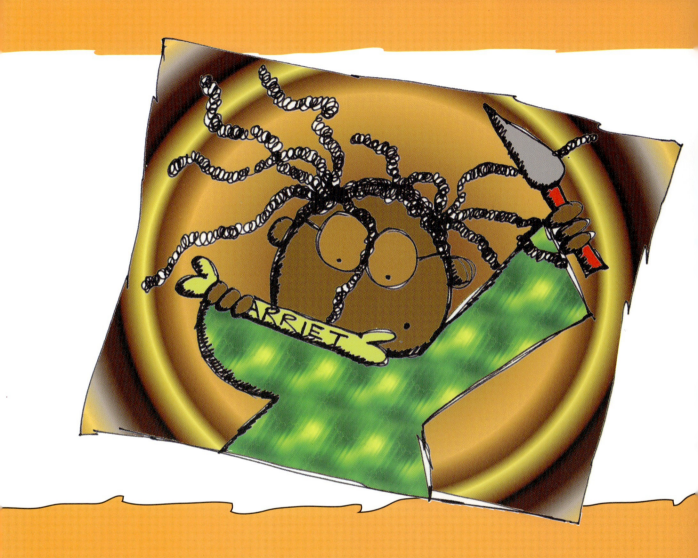

"I'm going to collect bones the rest of my life."
And she manically carved on her name, with a knife.

Soon she was hunting down bones from all over.
She dug up the bones of her dead dog called Rover.

The bones of her cat, and her last frog called Hoppy,
soon appeared next to her old rabbit, Floppy.

Next came the dentist, to buy tooth extractions,
but manky old teeth were just minor distractions...

Compared to her internet buy – yes, just wait,
a genuine angel-bone, found by a saint!

The house was soon filled, and the bones lay about.
Eventually, Harriet's parents moved out.

They stayed in a caravan parked round the back
to make room for Harriet's bones from a yak.

Six wildebeest were in each upper room.
Yes, Harriet's house was just one great big tomb!

One day she popped to the van, to see Mum,
and one paper headline made Harriet go numb.
"DINOSAUR SKELETON GONE UP FOR SALE!"
The bones on this thing were as big as a whale!

"I must have that dinosaur!" Harriet screamed.
"My small bones are suddenly not what they seemed.
I've searched my whole life for some sense of direction,
and those bones are it – I'VE FOUND BONE PERFECTION!"

Instantly, Harriet sold all her bones.

She sold off her bed, and her three mobile phones.

She sold off the wardrobe, and all of her fashion.

The dinosaur was now her ultimate passion.

When all that remained were the books by the loo,
she went onto ebay, and sold them off too.

Finally, wheeling a barrow of cash,
she ran from the house in a maddening dash...

Right to the place where the dinosaur stood.
She looked at her dino, and saw it was good!

So Harriet gave all she had for the bones.
A very wise girl was that Petrifee Jones.

If you found that one thing – the one thing that's true,
would you give your whole life to have it? Would you?

Matthew 13:44–46

The kingdom of heaven is like what happens when someone finds treasure hidden in a field and buries it again. A person like that is happy and goes and sells everything in order to buy that field.

The kingdom of heaven is like what happens when a shop owner is looking for fine pearls. After finding a very valuable one, the owner goes and sells everything in order to buy that pearl.

Try these activities out to explore the Bible passage more!

Worship

What you need
- Balloons
- CD player
- *Reach Up!* CD or other children's worship CD

What you do
Share out the balloons and help your child(ren) blow them up and tie a knot in them, if you need to. Together, write one word on each balloon which describes how you and your child(ren) feel about belonging to God (for example: safe, loved, happy, forgiven).

Play a lively song (for example: 'Wow!' from *Reach Up!*) and ask your child(ren) to pat their balloons so they are kept afloat in the air. Every time they pat a balloon invite them to shout out the word written on it.

Make and pray

What you need
- A small box each (food packaging or larger matchboxes with the sandpaper removed are ideal)
- Materials to decorate the boxes
- Felt-tip pens or crayons
- Glue stick

What you do
Tell your child(ren) that you're going to make treasure chests. Give your child(ren) a box and ask them to draw precious things on the outside and decorate it with the materials you have gathered together. Chat together about things that are important to you. Remind your child(ren) that the pearl was the greatest treasure to the person in the story. On the bottom of the inside, write 'Belonging to God' – this is the greatest treasure of all!

All hold your treasure chests and think about the people and things that are important to you. Together, imagine taking each of these things out of the treasure chest so that only 'Belonging to God' is left. Say a prayer thanking God that, even if our precious things were gone, we would still belong to him. (If the children find it hard to imagine, they could write or draw the important things on small pieces of paper.)

Sorting game

What you need

- Small pieces of card
- Felt-tip pens
- A card saying, 'Belonging to God'

What you do

Together, think of as many things that are important to you as you can. Write or draw each one on a separate piece of card. When you have finished, put the cards into order, starting with the most important and ending with the least – try to agree together on each one!

Ask your child(ren) whether each of your things might be the one that Jesus is talking about in the story. Hopefully they will say 'no'. Finally show a card saying 'Belonging to God' – is this the most important thing?

Chat

What you do

Talk with your child(ren) about the person in the story: what was the most important thing to them and what did they do to get it? Chat about what the most important thing for us should be. You may need to explain that having God as your friend is the most important thing. How easy is it to make other things more important than knowing God? Perhaps they are always busy with their toys, books, TV or homework and forget to pray to God or read the Bible. Maybe sometimes they don't want to come to church but would rather play football or go to visit their friends. You might like to share some struggles from your own life to help them realise that adults sometimes forget to make belonging to God the most important thing too!

Other titles by the same author

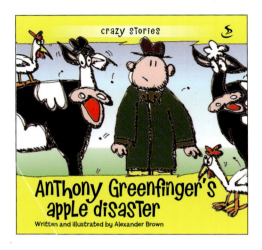

Anthony Greenfinger's apple disaster

Anthony Greenfinger is a farmer. He loves his chickens, his cows and the fleas but he longs for one more thing: apples! He sets out to plant apple trees but things don't go quite according to plan when he makes a very silly mistake!

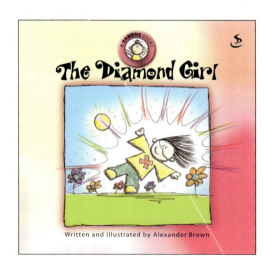

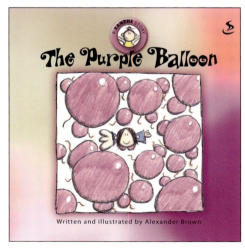

Order a copy at your local Christian bookshop or from : Scripture Union Mail Order, PO Box 5148, Milton Keynes MLO MK2 2YX. Tel: 0845 0706006. www.scriptureunion.org.uk